Look and Find®

RUDOLPH
THE
RED-NOSED REINDEER®

pi kids® publications international, ltd.

Why, hello! I am Sam the Snowman and this wintry wonderland is Christmastown. Everyone here is busy decorating for Christmas. Can you spot these ornaments that have been hung to bring Christmas cheer?

Silver star

Blue ball

Santa

Orange goldfish

A red-nosed reindeer

Green pickle

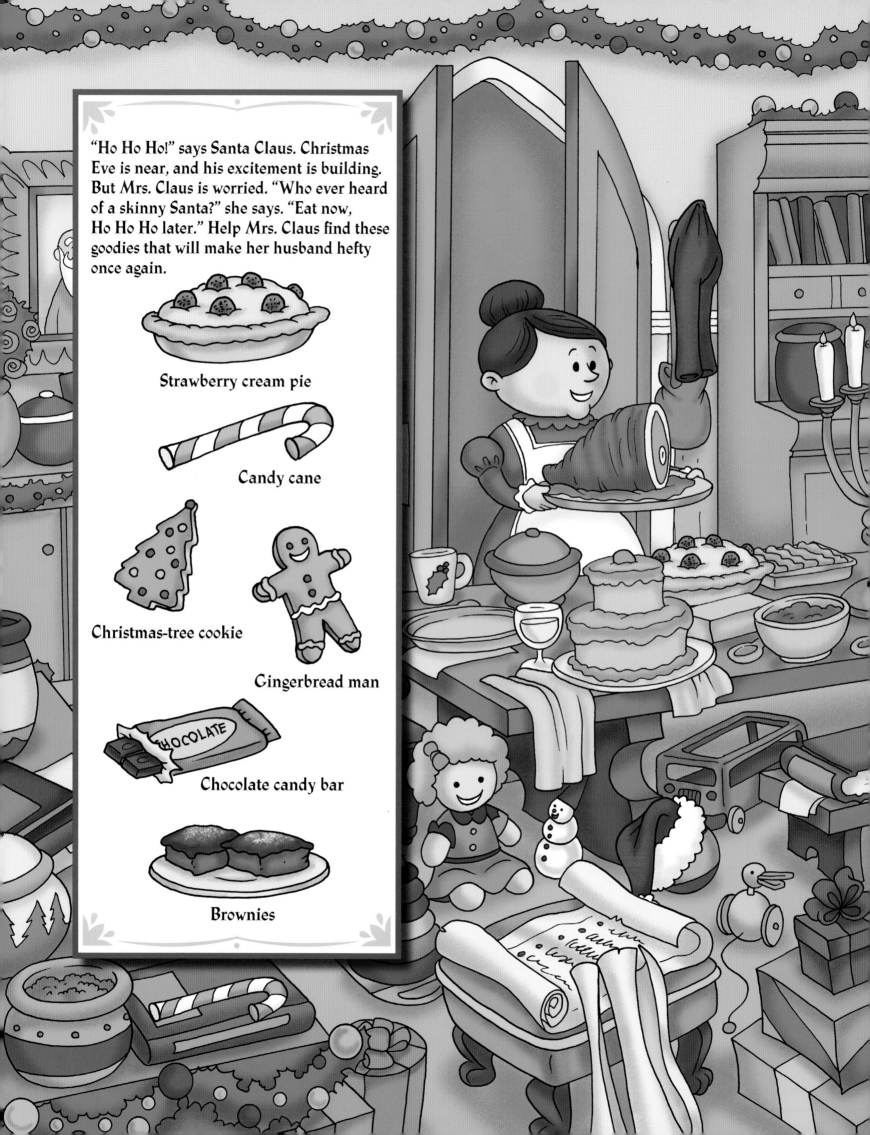

"Ho Ho Ho!" says Santa Claus. Christmas Eve is near, and his excitement is building. But Mrs. Claus is worried. "Who ever heard of a skinny Santa?" she says. "Eat now, Ho Ho Ho later." Help Mrs. Claus find these goodies that will make her husband hefty once again.

Strawberry cream pie

Candy cane

Christmas-tree cookie

Gingerbread man

Chocolate candy bar

Brownies

All of Santa's elves are busy making toys for Christmas—all except one. Hermey is an elf who doesn't want to make toys. He wants to be a dentist! Look around Santa's workshop for these dental tools that might help Hermey with his dream.

Drill

Scraper

Toothbrush

Dentures

Mirror

DENTISTRY

Dentistry book

It's time for the Reindeer Games! Rudolph and his pal Fireball are ready to show that they have what it takes to someday pull Santa's sleigh. Rudolph would also like to impress the pretty young reindeer Clarice. Look for these three and other characters as the young reindeer prepare to fly.

Clarice

Comet

Santa

Rudolph

Fireball

Donner

Rudolph and Hermey have run away because they feel like misfits. On the way, they meet Yukon Cornelius, a rough-and-tumble prospector. But the three friends had better be careful, the fearsome Bumble is after them! See if you can help them escape the Bumble by making your way through this icy maze.

THIN ICE

Our lovable gang of misfits has found a place where they hope to fit in — the Island of Misfit Toys. Find some of these characters who live on the island.

Spotted elephant

Charlie-in-the-box

Swimming bird

King Moonracer

Dolly

Train with square wheels

Having escaped the Bumble, Rudolph and Hermey are safely back home in Christmastown — and they've brought some new friends! It's time for Santa's annual flight, but the weather is awful foggy. Can you find who might be able to help Santa find his way? Then find these other characters who are ready for Christmas, too.

Hermey

Rudolph

Aviator Elf

Mrs. Claus

Clarice

Boss Elf

Merry Christmas! Rudolph is guiding Santa's sleigh through the fog, so that Santa can give gifts to the good girls and boys around the world. And thanks to Santa and Rudolph, the Misfit Toys will at last find loving homes. Find these Misfit Toys that Santa is delivering.

Spotted elephant

Dolly

Charlie

Winged bear

Bird

Train

They say no two snowflakes are alike. But head back to Christmastown and see if you can find six matching pairs.

Climb back into Mrs. Claus' kitchen and find these pieces of Santa's special suit.

Hat

Belt

Coat

Pants

Boots

Suspenders

Sneak back into Santa's workshop and look for these toys that will go to good girls and boys on Christmas morning.

This doll

This train

This car

This wagon

A toy soldier

A bicycle

Fly back to the Reindeer Games and look for these hidden forest animals.

This raccoon

This bunny

This bird

This squirrel

Bumble

Fish

Sled back to the escape from the Bumble and look for these frozen things that Yukon Cornelius dropped along the way.

Hat

Axe

Ear muffs

Sled

Pick

Snowshoes

Return to the Island of Misfit Toys and find these other mixed-up toys that live there.

A pink fire engine

A water pistol that squirts jelly

A cowboy riding an ostrich

A scooter for Jimmy

A boat that won't stay afloat

An airplane that can't fly

A bear on a bike

Land back in Christmastown and help Yukon Cornelius dig up 29 candy canes.

Rudolph's red nose saved the day. Return to Christmas Eve and find these other red things hidden around the scene.

Stop sign

Fire engine

A red flag atop a building

The cowboy's red ostrich

Stop light

A red barn